Anatomy of Violence

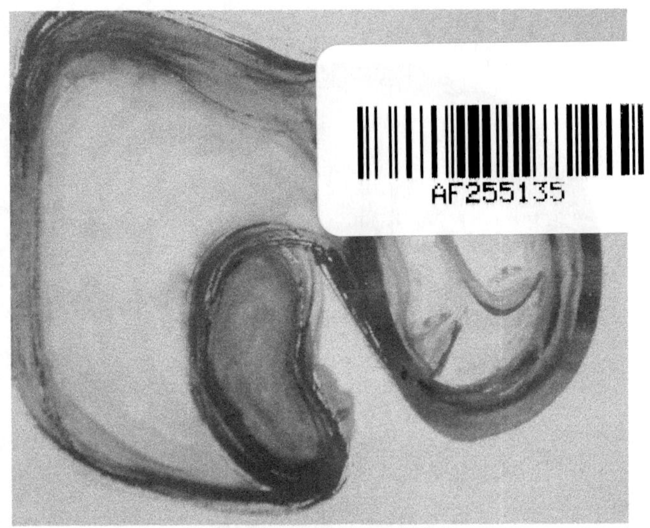

a slightly fictional story

By Dale Albert Johnson

Anatomy of Violence: An American Story

ISBN 978-1-300-43531-0

First Edition

Manufactured in the United States of America

New Sinai Press

Table of Contents

Cover Photo Credit:

Xia Peixian 夏沛仙

Painting by

Dale Albert Johnson

Anatomy of Violence:
An American Story

This is a book about seven generations of a family named Vandenbrugen. Their stories and lives are based on my family genealogy I have recently discovered. I was taken away from this family, after having been abandoned with my infant brother sixty years ago. My name was changed and any contact with my former family was broken. I grew up in a good and loving home which gave me a good start in life. My life would have taken a very different turn if I had remained in my birth family. I have no doubt that I would have continued the family psycho-pathology that expressed itself in violence and abuse.

I write this book because I am grateful, grateful to have broken the line of transmission of suffering and pain. This has happened by no act of my own. It was the courage and love of others whose intervention gave me a second life. It is this second life that I know well and have recorded in an autobiography. My first life, the life I was born into, is the life I can only imagine, yet it is a life anchored by facts. These facts come from census records, city directories, birth announcements, obituaries, genealogical records, and history books.

Because there is so much information that has been lost or never recorded I can only write the account in the form of a novel. But, because there is so much that is known this gives me a chance to write this book as a form of experimental fiction.

I have included footnotes, typical of a non-fiction account and combined documented facts with imagined dialogues and events. In a sense I have placed living facts within the body of fiction. For want of a term or phrase, I call this Zombie Literature.

This is a work of the living dead. I have attempted to take the true genealogical record of the Vandenburg family, my biological family, and used it to form the skeleton of the fictional Vandenbrugen story. Within the characters of the Vandenbrugen family are the real lives of the Vandenburg generations.

I have grown a fictional skin around the body of genealogical facts in my mental laboratory of experimental writing.

Writing a work of the imagination does distort the historical facts. The need to create dialogue and context requires guesswork. In the end nothing is completely true in this book although everything is fundamentally true.

I hope that people who read this will see a true story about the horror of inter-generational violence and how lives are destroyed, and happiness abandoned, and human hearts remain homeless. At the same time, I hope the reader will see a story of redemption and salvation even though it takes generations. I hope the reader will read a story that uses fiction to reveal a deeper and universal story of violence as an expression of self-hatred, mental illness, and intergenerational suffering that only requires love to break its hold on a family.

Dale Albert Johnson
born as
Lyle Francis Vandenburg Jr. son of Lyle Vandenburg, son of Paul Burchard Vandenburg, son of Jesse Keller Vandenburg, son of Martin Vandenburg, son of John Vandenburg, son of Cornelius Vandenburg.

New Year's Day 2014
Wuzhong, Ningxia, China

Chapter I: Origins

A violent man is a danger but a violent woman is a horror. Seven generations of my family have been victims of abuse of all kinds: self-abuse, sexual abuse, neglect, and outright violence. Ours is an American family!

As far as I can tell, the effects of violence on generations of our family began when Cornelius Vandenbrugen landed in America. He traveled to Albany where troops of Dutch farmers had fought in the French-Indian Wars. This was his baptism into the American experience. He settled into the Albany region and later fought in the War of Independence in 1777 when Dutch farmers like himself went to reinforce Americans fighting in the Battle of Saratoga. After the War of Independence he returned again to his farm and raised a family that included John Vandenbrugen who was born in 1796 and fought in the War of 1812 as a boy soldier of 17 years. John fought in the Battle for Plattsburgh September 11, 1813 as part of a ragtag group of irregulars made up of boys, invalids, and men unfit for duty. They saw their share of the horrors of war as they protected the hospital where wounded and maimed were sent behind the battle lines. Somehow this group of misfits saved Plattsburgh and helped to win the war for Lake Champlain and the American side of the Saint Lawrence Seaway.

John returned to life on the farm in south Albany and raised his family which included his son Martin. It was Martin who began a restless migration across America to escape the ravages of war. In Martin's case it was the Civil War that faced his generation. He wanted nothing to do with the War between the States. Instead of avoiding war he ended up in Eastern Kansas in the heart of pre-Civil War strife.

As far as I can tell, after three generations of war weary Vandenbrugen men, the violence turned inward in the family of Jesse Vandenbrugen, son of Martin. He married a woman who initiated generations of violence. His wife, Mary Jane, damned her children with brutal beatings making them the carriers of an inter-generational disease.

At a deeper level we have to ask why did Mary Jane marry Jesse Vandenbrugen? Her need to carry out violent acts against her children required a certain kind of man….a man like Jesse Vandenbrugen.

This recipe for inter-generational violence does not occur accidentally. It requires specific ingredients.

Jesse was the youngest member of a family of Dutch origin. He was a descendent of Calvinist people who believed in the utter depravity of human beings. This theology was expressed in cruel child-rearing practices by any standard. Children had to be beaten to "break the will" Which disciplines the natural sinfulness. John Calvin expressly stated that we are born sinners.

John Calvin believed that, because of Adam's disobedience in the Garden of Eden, the entire human race became essentially bad or immoral.[1] And because of this immoral character, Calvin continued, humans were incapable of doing any good of their own design.

The leading proponents of the Calvinistic view in Colonial America were people who wanted to purify the Church of England. Their religious belief that humans were essentially immoral had an impact upon their child-rearing practices and upon their educational philosophies. For example, because they believed children to be innately vile, they "did not hesitate to nourish them with threats, moralizing and the whip" (2)

If this theological view was combined with certain forms of mental illness, it could be a deadly combination and at the very least a sadist formula whose victims were vulnerable and had few defenses. Those children who survived such savagery were perfect companions for brutal men and woman of the next generation. In my case, it was the women who transmitted the intergenerational violence.

I know nothing about the wife of Martin Vandenbrugen, Martin's mother, except that her name was Isabella Catherine Keller. This is a name that is more likely Roman Catholic than Calvinist. It suggests that there may have been disharmony in the home and battles over child rearing practices. It is only speculation, but Jesse may have been a victim of such conflict under the domination of his mother. This made him a perfect candidate for Mary Jane who had to have some level of co-dependence from her husband.

Jesse's birth order may have also been a factor is the development of the relationship between Mary Jane Stewart and himself. Jesse was the youngest of six children. Women controlled his life. His older sisters naturally dominated him. At some level of unconsciousness as the "baby" of the family he was looking for someone who could take care of him.

Jesse and Mary Jane were a deadly match. Their marriage and their crimes lies at the heart of this story.

1. Dillenburger, J. 1975. *Calvin: Selected Writings.* Missoula, MT: Scholars' Press.
2. Thomas, R. 1979- *Comparing Theories of Child Development.* Belmont: Wadsworth.

Chapter II: Cornelius

Oh for a lodge in some vast wilderness
some boundless contiguity of shade
where rumor of oppression and deceit
of unsuccessful or successful war
might reach me no more

William Cowper

The English poet had once lived in 1689 on the East side of the Hudson not too far from where the first Vandenbrugen settled, up river near where Henry Hudson' Dutch passengers established a colony. Cowper's dream of an ancient and primitive forest that would somehow romantically protects it's settlers from violence did not come true.

The first Vandenbrugen to arrive in America was Jesse's great-grandfather, Cornelius, who arrived in the harbor of New York as a child sometime in   early 1760. New York had once been named New Amsterdam so it seemed as if it would be a place for the Vandenbrugen's from Holland.   But, the English had taken it from the Dutch 100 years earlier. Still there was a strong presence of the Dutch in the city. Nevertheless, it did not take long before the family of Cornelius Vandenbrugen felt the unwelcome prejudice of the English majority.

They took a vessel up the Hudson River to a Dutch colony of Schodack that was settled by the Dutch soon after Henry Hudson's exploration of the Hudson River in 1609. Before the Dutch came, the land was farmed and hunted by Indians of the Mohican tribe. The hamlet of Schodack Landing was an early center of river trade and part of the Albany region. It was 170 miles west of Boston and 150 miles north of New York.

It was also a land taken by violence. This region of upstate New York, directly west of Boston, was the site of bloody battles. Dutch farmers of Albany region fought and murdered the Native Americans who had little chance with the French on one side and the Dutch farmers on the other.

Later in 1777 these same Dutch men took up arms including pitchforks in some cases after the battle of Lexington and fought the British at Saratoga. Cornelius fought in Van Corlandt's

New York Regiment under the command of Major General Benedict Arnold. Horatio Gates wrote a letter to General George Washington describing the bloody fights by American farmer soldiers which included Cornelius.

More than 3500 British and German soldiers were wounded or killed. Among them Brigadier Simon Frazer was mortally wounded. British messengers, who were sent with messages to other British regiments, were captured and hanged. The lack of communication with other British regiments and the overwhelming force by the Americans who outnumbered the British by 3 to 1 led to the British defeat at Saratoga.

On the American side Benedict Arnold was wounded in the Battle at Freeman's farm. Nevertheless he heroically battled on and captured supplies heading to the British troops. It was a bloody battle.

It is the young who see the worst violence of any war.

This was a land bought with blood and born out of violence. It was a nexus point of fear. British, French, Mohican natives all fought for this tiny area of land.

Early court records in Albany point to conflicting views on who owned the land. Early Dutch settlers testified that they purchased the land with fur pelts, produce, silver, and even cloth. The natives disagreed. Many of them testified that the land was only leased. The courts ruled against the natives by often creating legislation that backdated claims and issued deeds that were never signed by the native tribal representatives.

In the post war period, Cornelius and other farmer soldiers returned to their farms, built towns, and organized local governments. The towns of Ressenlaer County were not only of Dutch origin but they were slaves holders. Census records at the turn of the century (1801) reveals that the village of Shodack had 151 slaves and 298 free whites. There was one slave for every two whites.

A report in the Troy News (Albany's Newspaper) stated the following:

"When a child was born of a negro woman, at the age of three it was presently to person of the owner's family of the same gender.   The owner's family member would present and envelope of money and shoes to the Negro mother."

How horrifying this must hast been for the slave mother. All she got in return was a tiny about of money and baby shoes by which to remember the child.

Furthermore if the slave grew up to be rebellious, refusing to do his or her duties the slave was sold to an owner in Jamaica.

Did Cornelius own slaves? It is possible he did own slaves to work on his farm although there is no record of it. He certainly saw them bought and sold and publicly punished in the town square. Every town of Ressenlaer County contained rules and regulations for the public whipping of slaves in the town square. It regulated how much to pay to whipper (no more than 4 pence per head), how many lashes for each offense, and the size and construction of the stockade.

In 1799 laws were passed that would end slavery in Ressenlaer County. It was decreed that any child born of a slave would be free after they served a period 27 years (male) or 25 years (female).

This society of people who endured war, owned slaves, battled nature and their neighbors, read the Bible and Calvin's Institutes.

What kind of people do these experiences and influences produce? What happens in families who occupy land they have gained by deceit and stealth? How do the women deal with the daily fear of attack? How do children cope with threats to beat the hell out of them? What does the fatigue of war do to the men who kill and are nearly killed? The answers are as complex as the human condition. Some families cope by perpetuating the climate of violence. Others are tempered like hardened steel. Some transcend the anger and hatred and find peace in their hearts. Others move on and on in a restless struggle to escape the pain. The Vandenbrugen families were shaped by these early brutal experiences and were shaped by them in the following generations.

It was only a matter of time before the external conflicts turned inward. This is a function of violence. It creates people who become addicted to the blood lust. When external enemies disappear as seen through the lenses of patriotism and honor the war turns inward. Men and women are left with visions of horrors, and feelings of guilt, and regret. The expurgation of the pain is often found in drink and drugs, or worse, by lashing out at one's own kin, hidden behind the view of privacy. This expurgation can sometimes takes generations to work out.

Cornelius bought land from the native Mohican families. He planted apple trees forming a small orchard. The seed of the violence he had seen and executed was still buried within him. It would take a few more generations before the true hell of which he was a part would be expressed. He began a family in Schodack that included John.

Note:
Actual court records and public accounts for this chapter are drawn from *A History of Ressenlaer County, Colonization of the Manor of Ressenlaerwyke to the present time*, A. J. Wese, 1880.

Chapter III: John (1796

John was 16 years old when the War of 1812 broke out. He was recruited the following year to assist in the Battle for Plattsburgh. It could not have happened at a worse time. The apple harvest was about to begin. John was becoming an important worker in the harvest. Nevertheless, he was conscripted into the Northern Army under the command of General Izard.

General George Izard was the son of a member of the Continental Congress, Ralph Izard. His mother was a niece of a Governor of New York, Alice De Lancey.

George Izard grew up in privilege and access to education in the finest schools in Philadelphia, Germany, and France.

John was sworn into the army by General Izard and then immediately assigned to the military hospital at Plattsburgh.   The Americans lacked training. The British knew this to be the vulnerability of the Americans. Given the late season British General Provost decided to invade New York State. His army outnumbered the American defenders of Plattsburgh. John Vandenbrugen was called to the front and was a member of the defenders of Plattsburgh. Prevost was worried about his flanks so he decided he needed the naval control of Lake Champlain. On the lake, the British squadron under Captain Geoge Downie and the Americans under Master Commandant Thomas Macdonough were more evenly matched.

On reaching Plattsburgh, Prevost delayed the assault until Downey arrived in a hastily built 36-gun frigate HMS *Confiance.*

Prevost forced Downie to attack before the ship was technologically ready or properly supplied. Prevost then unaccountably failed to provide the promised military support.

John and his fellow recruits were rushed out of the hospital dormitories and manned to cannons on the shore of Plattsburgh Bay. At first it was like an even chess game. But to their surprise the HMS Confiance ran out of ammunition. At the same time the wind died and the vessel was stranded and vulnerble to attack. The cannons fired from the American shore. John was rendered deaf in his left ear from the thunder of the cannons. He did not even notice the blood streaming down his neck. He was whooping and hollering with his fellow soldiers because the vessel was foundering and it was reported that the British Commander was killed.

Downie was killed and his naval force defeated at the naval Battle of Plattsburgh in Plattsburgh Bay on September 11, 1814.

The Americans now had control of Lake Champlain. President Teddy Roosevelt later called it "the greatest naval battle of the war." A successful land defense was led by Alexander McComb. Prevost then turned back in retreat, saying it would be too hazardous to remain on enemy territory after the loss of naval supremacy.

Prevost was recalled and in London, a naval court-martial decided that defeat had been caused principally by Prevost.

John returned to the farm in Shodack. The orchard was in ruins.   His father was unable to bring in the full crop. It took years for the farm to recover. John raised a family on the farm which included a son Martin.

Chapter IV: Martin (1832-1912)

Martin was apprenticed to a wood worker. He learned to make furniture. With this skill he was able to save enough money so at age 29 he moved west to Jefferson, County Kansas.

"Martin, I hear you are leaving us?" It was a neighbor farmer on the doorstep of Martin's house.

"Yes, I am heading to Kansas" Martin grinned.

"But why?"

"Frankly I don't want to get involved in the war between the States. Virginia is about to vote and secede from the Union. Those southern boys do not like to be told what to do. It has come to war. The use of violence to change men's minds never works."

"It has never worked before. I do not see how it will work now!" said Martin emphatically.

Both men were silent for a few minutes. Then Martin spoke up. "The only thing this violence can do is change behaviors and often it is not the way you expect. War is a terrible thing. I do not see how a good God can condone war."

"The Bible is full of war. The Battle of Jericho gave the Chosen People their land. Don't you think God is on the side of the right?"

"No, I do not sir. Right and wrong are the ideas of human beings and they are mostly wrong about such notions. God is on the side of those whom the world considers weak....those who flee from fights. God is on the side of those whom the world consider poor in spirit...who show humility and seek the cause of peacemakers. This is why I am going west. I have no desire for war, no desire for notions of right and wrong to the exclusion of compromise and compassion. The coming war will only bring more suffering, injustice, and misery. I will have none of it."

Martin moved to the border region in the 1850s. He appears on the 1860 census list. It is likely he was assisted in his move by the New England Emigrant Aid Company (est.1854) created to transport immigrants to the Kansas Territory to shift the balance of power so that Kansas would enter the United States as a free state rather than a slave state. The Company was created by Eli Thayer in the wake of the Kansas-Nebraska Act, which allowed the population of Kansas Territory to choose whether slavery would be legal or not. The Company is noted for the political impact it had on proslavery and antislavery movement. Thayer's prediction that the Company would eventually be able to send 20,000 immigrants a year turned out to be mere hyperbole.

Instead it spurred Border Ruffians from nearby Missouri, where slavery was legal, to move to Kansas in order to ensure its admission to the Union as a slave state. This in turn further motivated Free-Staters and enemies of "The Slave Powers" to act and support immigrants from New England such as Martin.

Thayer's intention was pecuniary and a brazen attempt to capitalize on antislavery sentiment in the Northern United States and send settlers to

Kansas to purchase land and build houses, shops and mills. They could then sell the land at a significant profit and send the proceeds back to Thayer and his investors. Several investors found the notion of profiting from the antislavery cause distasteful and perhaps immoral. The Company was transformed into a charity and it was renamed the New England Emigrant Aid Company in 1855. While the Company achieved neither a profit nor a significant impact on the population of Kansas, it played an important role in the events that would later be termed Bleeding Kansas.

The company was directly responsible for creating the Kansas towns of Lawrence and Manhattan, and it played a key role in founding Topeka and Osawatomie. Lawrence was named after the Company secretary, Amos Lawrence. Many politicians emerged in the emigrants who left for Kansas, such as Martin F. Conway, who would later be Kansas's first U.S. Representative.

The exact number of people who left for Kansas is unknown. James Rawley puts the numbers somewhere around 2000, of whom about a third returned home.

Martin landed in eastern Kansas during a

dangerous period of pre-Civil War battles. For a man who wanted to avoid war he landed in the middle of a battle.

There were a few skirmishes related to the Civil War in Eastern Kansas. Lawrence Kansas was nearly completely destroyed in some of the battles along the Kansas/Missouri border.

Bloody Kansas or the Border War was a series of violent political confrontations involving anti-slavery Free-Staters and pro-slavery "Border Ruffian" elements, that took place in the Kansas Territory and the neighboring towns of Missouri between 1854 and 1861. At the heart of the conflict was the question of whether Kansas would enter the Union as a free state or slave state. As such, Bleeding Kansas was a proxy war between Northerners and Southerners over the issue of slavery in the United States. The term "Bleeding Kansas" was coined by Horace Greeley of the *New York Tribune*; the events it encompasses directly presaged the American Civil War, as well as the future relationship between Kansas and Missouri.

Congress had long struggled to balance the interests of pro- and anti-slavery forces. The events later known as Bleeding Kansas were set into motion by the Kansas–Nebraska Act of

1854, which nullified the Missouri Compromise and instead implemented the concept of popular sovereignty. A "States-Rights" idea, popular sovereignty stated that the inhabitants of each territory or state should decide whether it would be a free or slave state; however, this resulted in immigration *en masse* to Kansas by activists from both sides. At one point, Kansas had two separate governments, each with its own constitution, although only one was federally recognized. On January 29, 1861, Kansas was admitted to the Union.

After the Civil War Kansas filled up with survivors of the violent struggle to preserve the Union. Violence created violent people. Former soldiers took out their aggression on Buffalo and Native Americans. There was an entire generation of men with post traumatic disorder...men prone to acts of self-hatred and a need to purge themselves of painful memories. In those days these psychological wounds were called "Soldiers heart." Martin started his family in Kansas Territory. He wasted no time in building a family of six children. They lived in the town of Grasshopper Falls west of Kansas City and north of Topeka in the region of eastern Kansas.

Chapter V: Jesse

The youngest boy of the Martin Vandenbrugen family was Jesse born in 1874. He and his older brother, Dow, were inseparable. There was not a tree they did not climb, a mud puddle they did not attack, nor a class at school they did not skip. They were night and day. Jesse was fire. Dow was water. Because Dow was older he could calm the impulsiveness of his brother. As teenagers they heard of the fortunes they could make in the gold fields of Colorado. In the town of Delaware was a man who returned from the Gold Rush of '49 in California. He built the largest house in town. It was called "the Mansion." Jesse had once broken into it not to steal anything but to just look around. For this act he got a severe beating from his father. It was the last time his father ever laid a hand on him. Jesse ran away from home that night. He returned to "the Mansion" and stole cash he had seen in a jewelry box in the master bedroom.

When Jesse arrived in Pike's Peak newspapers were full of detail about Lizzie Borden who was accused of murdering her parents with an ax. It was on Aug. 4, 1892, a sultry summer day, that Andrew and Abby Borden were brutally murdered in their 92 Second St. home.

Abby, lifeless, was photographed lying face down on a dark floral carpet in the guest bedroom. Her soles pointing up and her skirts barely ruffled, she was situated between the bed and bureau. The woman had been struck 19 times by a hatchet.

Downstairs, her husband, Andrew, was also dead, presumably killed with 11 blows from the same hatchet while he napped on the sofa. He is pictured wearing a business suit, despite the August heat, and has bent knees and both feet on the floor.

Anyone who's ever seen the crime scene photographs would believe the bodies were discovered in those exact positions. But excerpts discovered by the Fall River Historical Society in the journals of Attorney Andrew Jackson Jennings, hand-written after the murders of Abby and Andrew Borden, tell a very different story.

Before Abby was photographed, the bed was moved and her body was "rolled over and set up" while authorities examined her head, according to Jennings' interview of Dr. Seabury Bowen, a physician who lived across the street from the Bordens and was called to the scene the day of the murders.

Bowen told Jennings he found her "lying perfectly still with both arms under her." He said her head was a "couple feet from the mop-board." Whoever killed her hit her hear 19 times with a hatchet. A hatchet hear was found in the basement with no handle. Lizzie's father was hit 11 times. One blow severed in two his eyeball. It was a brutal and vicious murder. What made the crime even more suspicious was that Lizzie admitted to burning a dress in the stove. She said she had gotten paint on it.

The jury acquitted her after less than two hours deliberation. There was not enough physical evidence to link her to the crime.

Popular opinion believed that Lizzie was guilty of murder. The motive was money and Lizzie benefited from her father's death. After the acquittal Lizzie and her sister bought a new house. Lizzie remained in their home town for the remainder of her life.

In a sense, this changed America's view of women. Women could be a danger to men or their   children.

The idea that a woman could commit such murders and carry out such heinous acts of violence shook the psyche of America. Jesse hated his mother. He never saw her again after he left home. In a strange way the Lizzie Borden case gave Jesse even more reason to justify his escape from home as a teenager.

Dow caught up to his brother a year later at the train station in Pike's Peak, Colorado. Jesse was living in a boarding house. He had staked out a claim in nearby Anaconda. He found copper ore but no gold. Jesse had received a letter from his brother who was very worried about him. Jesse was at the railroad station when his brother stepped off the train. There may have even been a tear in his eye. Jesse swaggered up to his brother. "Ah, my brother's keeper. How are you Dow?"

Dow hugged Jesse. "Have you struck it rich?"

"Not yet, not yet. Let me get your bags. We are going to celebrate."

Jesse grabbed Dow bags and strode through the station house and out the other side and onto a dusty street. It was 1892. Ellis Island reception center had opened. It was the beginning of the immigrant era. Fredrick Turner had published his famous essay announcing the end of the frontier in America. Jesse and Dow could not have begun their adventure at a worse time. A flood of new immigrants had already arrived in the boom town of Pike's Peak. Jesse and Dow heard a number of languages on their way to the boarding hose: Norwegian, German, French, Spanish, Swedish, and Italian.

Jesse climbed two flights of stairs with Dow's bags. He refused to let Dow carry even one. Jesse kicked open a door and threw the bags in a corner. "You can sleep on the floor if you like. I will get you a bed tomorrow. Let's go celebrate!"

Jesse went out the door and bounded down the stairs. Dow followed him outside. A heavy door stood open. A German scene was carved into the wood featuring a stag in an Alpine forest.

"Jesse"shouted Dow. He heard "Over here brother. Meet my friends." Jesse already had a couple of drinks poured."

"What is it?" Dow asked.

"Brandy." Jesse was gleeful.

Alcohol was not allowed in the house of their parents except at Christmas and special occasions. Their father, Martin, and their mother Isabella followed the pious pattern of the Dutch Protestants. Jesse and Dow's great grand-father left the Netherlands as a part of a great Protestant migration to America. Catholic estate owners controlled land and jobs. An excess population of Protestant Dutch citizens leaded for America, a land of opportunity and religious freedom. Theirs was an austere Calvinist faith of bare churches, plain altars, and pious homes. There was no work on Sundays. Silence and Bible reading was the rule. Children were beaten and punished for their own good and God's pleasure. The enemies were the Papists – the Roman Catholics.

The Calvinist principle of child-rearing in the 19th century depended upon breaking the will of the child. Children were seen as small adults. They were expected to work and contribute to the family income at age. 7. There certainly was not such a thing as adolescent. In America there were two views of child reading: the Calvinist view and the Romantic view. The Calvinist view was harsh and directed toward the redemption of the child who was born in sin. The latter view, the Romantic view, was advocated by Rousseau.

Two forces in the 17th and 18th centuries began to re-shape attitudes toward children. First, the Industrial Revolution had freed women from the land and daily work in the fields. She could now devote her time to the home and the care of children. Second, advances in reducing infant mortality allowed parents to invest more emotional attachments to their children. Nevertheless, harsh Calvinist practices were resistant to change.

Dow and Jesse were all too eager to rebel against their Protestant Dutch past.

Dow drank his brandy too fast. He coughed and teared up. Jesse laughed. After a few minutes Dow began to warm up.

"This is Samuel. He helps me pack gear. He is going up to the mine tomorrow. He says he will take us." Jesse was beaming.

"Where?" Dow seemed confused.

"To my mine. Actually my claim. I have not started mining yet. I still need to show results on pilot samples."

Samuel jumped into the conversation, "Yah, it looks real good. Your brother may hit it big. The assay in nearby mines shows color."

"What do you mean color?" Dow asked."

"Gold! You clod-head." Sam and Jesse laughed.

"Brother, the real money is in buying and selling claims. It costs a fortune to actually mine a claim. If I can prove my claim then I can sell it for a fortune."

"What do you mean 'prove it'?" Dow seemed

irritated now. "You are throwing around all these terms and they mean nothing to me.

"Settle down friend. Proving a claim means showing there is gold on the property and estimating the amount of gold on it." Sam took a potato out of his pocket. Dow laughed. "Is this lunch?"

"No, it is what we use to detect   gold. You see we take this vile of mercury and mix it with a small amount of ore we crush, Put it is the middle of the potato in a cavity we carve out. Then we cook it, open it up and 'wahlah' the gold has been drawn out."

"You see, the mercury attaches to the gold, separates it from the ore. The cooking evaporates the mercury and what you have left is the gold." Jesse said confidently.

"You mean if there is gold."

"We will   find out tomorrow. I am taking this potato and vile of mercury up to the site." Sam turned serious now. "This will change our lives."

Jesse and Dow returned to the boarding house next door. Jesse flopped onto his bed. Dow covered himself with a blanket on the floor. "Jesse, you awake?"

"Um" grunted Jesse. "Is this your claim ? What is in it for your friend Sam?"

"I promised him first option on the claim for help to prove the claim and transporting us up there."

"First option?"

"Yes, he is first in line to buy the claim."

The next day Sam pounded on the door. "Get up you bone-heads." We got a long ride.

Dow and Jesse threw on their clothes. Boots pounded the floor like hammers. "Quiet down." A voice could be heard from below. Jesse, Dow, and Sam moved down the stairs like jack rabbits to a chorus of voices: "Shutup!"

It took the entire day to travel from Pike's Peak to Teller mining camp. It was a rough collection of 49ers and 59ers. The 49ers were men who failed to find gold in California and were looking to a second chance in the gold rush of Colorado. The 59ers were men who had the gleam of gold in their eye and did not want to miss out on the American experience. Many were civil war veterans who left the madness of the Great War and went west for find their fortune. Gold was first found on the Upper Platte River in 1859, hence, the name 59ers. Most did not arrive until the late 1860's and 70s. Dow and Jesse were 20 years late. A generation had passed. Fortunes were made and spent. A minor gold rush occurred west of Pike's Peak at Cripple Creek in 1890 on the eastern slope of the Rockies. Teller was a last wish boom town. It was for dreamers and thieves and con men all hoping to prey upon one another for one last time. The mining camp grew from 500 to

10,000. It seemed as if Dow, Jesse, and Samuel were the last three men to arrive.

Jesse said to Dow, "We stay here tonight in the camp. First thing in the morning we head out to the claim."

"I'll follow you."

Tents were set up in a long line. Jesse went to the camp office. "Number 26." Dow followed Jesse down the muddy street. It was an Army tent. Jesse pointed to two bunks. He took the third. There were seven other bunks in the room. Another young man was sitting on his bunk. "Friend, can you tell us where to get some grub.

The young man stood up. He was as tall a Jesse. "Mess hall. I am going there myself. Want to come?"

"Sure, the boys and I haven't eaten all day." Jesse stretched out his hand. "Jesse

Vandenbrugen's the name."

"Henry Miller. Ready to go. Follow me."

"On the way to the dining hall Dow said "I heard your name was Miller. I just read a book on the train on my way out here by a fellow named Miller. Joaqin Miller."

"That's my father. What was the name of the book,   *My life Among the Modocs?*"

"Yes, that was it."

"Dam full of lies. My father does not know the truth from a hole in the ground."

"Are you telling me the truth? Your father really is Joaqin Miller?"

"Yup, he is in Oakland, California, right now telling all those miners who hit it big all his yarns."

"Really, it is all lies?"

"Well most of it. He did ride the pony express in Oregon. He was a judge out there until his past life of horse thieving caught up with him. He go to England and read his poems to all the people who would have believed he was another Kit Carson."

"He wrote in the book that he got   an arrow shot into his mouth and it turned him temporarily blind."

"Well, that is true too. Maybe...he does have a scar in the back of his neck. When they pulled it out he got his sight back."

"I would love to meet your Dad."

"I wouldn't wish it on my worst enemy."

Dow didn't say anything for a moment. "I'm sorry you feel that way about your father."

"Let's just drop it."

Jesse headed into the chow hall first. A man at the door grumbled. "Two bits each." He eyed the other boys enough so they dug into their pockets and handed the man their coins.

Jesse winked at a gal serving food. "This is my gal. What do you think of her? Her name's Mary Jane."

Dow and Samuel nodded respectfully at Mary Jane.

"I'll give you a beatin with this spoon if you aren't careful" Mary Jane waved a big spoon at Jesse. Jesse laughed and headed to a corner table.

"Is she really your gal Jesse?" Dow asked.

"Yup, I aim to make her my partner in fun."

The next morning Jesse, Dow, and Samuel heading up to their claim. They arrived in a tree lined area of a small stream bed. In the distance were a couple of major structures. "Looks like some of the big boys are operating here" Dow commented.

"Yah, the days of the small time operator are nearly over." Jesse bellowed from the creek side.

Jesse and Sam set up a sluice box, a grated slab-board with riffles over few inches. "As the water and   gavel passes over the riffles the heavier material catches behind the riffles. After about an hour of hard work wrestling the sluice box so it lined up with a small stream of water and shoveling hundreds and hundreds of pounds of gravel Jesse shouted. " got some color here." Dow and Samuel peered into the box Sure enough there was some color mixed in with black sand."

Jesse scraped up some material and gave the deposit to Samuel but Samuel shrugged off

Jesse.

"I got my own mixture here." Samuel who prepared a mixture of mercury with a sample of deposit material. He placed the amalgam in several potatoes and careful laid them in a fire pit he had prepared earlier.

After about an hour Samuel took the potatoes out. "Hot dam, gentlemen we have gold and I mean a lot of gold."

For a few minutes there was a lot of jumping and hollering. "Boys, boys, let us not attract attention. Let us get this back to camp. We have to file proof of claim and register the claim as a proven site. A lawyer friend of mine will draw up the papers.

Back at the camp Jesse instructed the others to lay low and not say a work. It was dangerous to mention a strike. People had been murdered over less. After a couple of days Jesse and Samuel were summoned to the lawyer's office.

"Gentlemen, you have a proven claim. I need to

ask either of you if you want to buy out the other man?   Jesse and Samuel looked at each other as the lawyer waited for a reply.

Jesse said, "I don't have a nickel to my name. I have no way to buy out Sam."

Sam shuffled in his seat. "Jesse, I have some family money. If we can agree on a price I might be able to buy out your share. I cannot offer a lot and you might have to discount your share but I am willing to talk.

It took a few days but Sam offered Jesse ten thousand dollars. It was a fortune to Jesse but according to the assay the mine was worth a hundred thousand time what Samuel offered. Jesse took the offer. After a week he had his money.

In the meantime Dow and Jesse waiting at the boarding house back at Pikes Peak. Jesse borrowed a small amount of money from his friend Henry Mark Miller. He gave him a notarized promissory note from the lawyer's office that he had the resources to repay the debt.

Henry Mark Miller met with Jesse and Dow at the Pike Hotel the day Jesse received payment. "What happened, did you make a strike. You boys have been very hush-hush about this money."

"Nah, just some family money" said Jesse with a poker face.

"I understand your friend Samuel has been working your claim and has not found anything yet. There is some talk you have cheated him. Did you sell him your claim?

Jesse was now visibly nervous. "Yes, I sold him my majority share but we found gold there I swear."

"That is not what he says."

Suddenly, Samuel appeared from the kitchen doorway. "I say you are a liar." Samuel pointed a gun at Jesse. Suddenly the kitchen door swung open knocking Samuel forward. The gun discharged missing Jesse. Jesse grabbed the gun that had fallen to the floor and ran out of the hotel with Dow following after him. For the next few weeks the brothers hid out in El Paso County.

Dow asked Jesse one day, "I have been wondering how you tricked Samuel."

"I switched the potatoes when Sam was busy with something else. I spiked a potato with a few flakes of gold."

Dow commented, "That area where you had a claim was known for another case of trickery. A mine was salted with gold and sold to an unsuspecting buyer. It made people suspicious of buying unproven claims."

"That is why I used the potato switch. By making Sam think he was determining the worth of the claim it gave him the confidence in the value. If that lawyer had not done another test we would have been in the clear."

Eventually things died down when Dow heard that Samuel discovered not gold but copper ore on his site.

Marcus Daly bought out Samuel's claim for a small fortune, enough to buy forgiveness to Jesse. The news of this fortune left Jesse bitter and determined to find his fortune and hit it big. If he could do it once he could do it again.

Anaconda Copper Mining Company started in 1881 when Marcus Daly bought a small silver mine called Anaconda near Butte, Montana. He asked George Hearst, father of publishing magnate William Randolph Hearst, for additional support. Hearst agreed to buy one-fourth of the new company's stock without visiting the site. Huge deposits of another mineral, copper, were discovered soon and Daly became a copper magnate. Daly quietly bought up neighboring mines including ones on Colorado forming a mining company. He then built a smelter at Anaconda which he connected to Butte by a railway.

Butte, as well as Pike's Peak, small and poor

towns, became one of the most prosperous cities in the country, often called "the Richest Hill on Earth." From 1892 through 1903, the Anaconda mine was the largest copper-producing mine in the world. It produced more than $300 billion worth of metal in its lifetime.

In 1889 the Rothschilds attempted to control the world copper market. In 1892 the French Rothschilds began negotiations to buy the Anaconda mine. In mid-October 1895 the Rothschilds, French and British, bought one quarter of the stock in Anaconda for 7.5 million dollars. This included the copper mines in Colorado. By the late 1890s the Rothschilds had control over the sale of about forty percent of the world's copper production.

The Rothschilds' role in Standard Oil Anaconda was brief. In 1899, Daly teamed up with two directors of John D. Rockefeller   to create the giant Amalgamated Copper Mining Company, one of the largest trusts of the early 20th century

By 1899 Amalgamated Copper acquired majority stock in the Anaconda Copper Company and the Rothschilds appear to have had no further role in the company. Marcus

Daly had just become president of the seventy-five million-dollar holding company at his death in 1900.

Marcus Daly died in 1900, and his widow began a close friendship with a shrewd, intelligent businessman, John D. Ryan, who assumed the presidency of Daly's bank and management of the widow's fortune.

Chapter VI : Mary Jane

Dow remained in El Paso County. He married Lorna Myrtle Montegue and together they raised a beautiful family that produced Arthur Vandenbrugen who became an important United States senator. An airbase in California is named after him.

Jesse met with Henry Mark Miller again. They discussed the Alaskan Gold Rush. Jesse figured there was too much competition. Besides it required a huge grub stake to go up there. Henry dropped a hint that a US Mint might be established in The Dalles, Oregon. To Jesse this meant that there was a huge deposit of gold in the area. Denver had established a mint because of the gold fields in Colorado. For whatever reason Jesse figured he could strike it big in Oregon.

In the meantime he met the love of his life at the mining camp. Mary Jane Stewart was a fireball at 4'8 and packed a punch of a man twice her size. She went to work in a mining camp in

Colorado not far from Pikes Peak. She had an eye on Jesse Vandenburg. Jesse was well practiced in the art of love. Women loved him and often saw him as a savior and a way out of the harshness of the mining camps.   At 6'3 he stood head and shoulders over Mary Jane. Their romance was a wild love affair. Other men in the camp in Teller could not help but notice this couple.

Mary Jane was a dark eyed teenager when Jesse met her. She was 14 years old when she entered the life of the gold mining camp. She certainly could not have had an easy life in the camp as a virgin girl among rough and wild men. Jesse was her protector but eventually succumbed to the call of love.

Jesse and Mary Jane raised a small family in Colorado Springs. Two children were born to them: Paul and Fred. Jesse was restless and missed his wild and single life.   Eventually they headed to Grant County in Oregon. Henry Mark Miller told him that his father was the former judge of the county. His wife was a Dyer and very influential in the history of Oregon. He was told, after gold was discovered in 1862 on Whiskey Flat, it has been estimated that within ten days 1,000 miners were camped along Canyon Creek. This increased population created a need for county government. Grant County's government was ratified in November 1857. It employs the old-western county government system: the County Court, with a County Judge and two Commissioners. The third man to serve as County Judge of Grant County was Cincinnatus Hiner "Joaquin" Miller (1837–1913) He was noted as a poet, playwright, and western naturalist and was called the "Poet of the Sierras" and the "Byron of the Rockies."

Jesse and Mary Jane Stewart married each other for all the wrong reasons. Jesse was a womanizer and had the wanderlust. He was gone for long periods of time. Mary Jane was a very frustrated woman. She described Jesse's dalliances as his "bad behavior." She beat her children without mercy. Paul and Fred were the victims of her abuse. She finally had enough of the dreams of her husband and left him. Money and riches were always about tomorrow, never today. The final straw for Mary Jane was when her husband moved the family to Grant County Oregon.

One day Jesse came home to his small family. Paul and Fred were school age and anxious to show their father school work they had just finished. Jesse blew past them and announced to his wife who kept her back to him while peeling potatoes at the kitchen sink.
"We are moving to Oregon."

"Oregon, where is Oregon?" said Fred.

"Shut up, your father is talking." Mary Jane turned and faced her husband with the potato peeler in her hand. "We are not going to Oregon. We can hardly afford our life here in Colorado. How we going to move a thousand miles away?"

"Don't worry dear. I have a tip on a gold strike. We'll be rich soon."

"Where are we going to get the money?" Mary Jane's face was red with anger.

"I borrowed money. We leave tomorrow."

Mary Jane burst into tears.

Mary Jane had taken to beating her children.

Her husband left the discipline up to his wife. Sometimes he would see serious marks on his boys. The boys reported being beiated, locked up, and having food and water withheld. When he asked Mary Jane about the abuse she often gave strange answers.

"I was told to beat them."

"Who told you?" Jesse quieried.

"The voice. I heard a voice telling me." Mary Jane's eyes seemed to turn darker. "The boys were on fire. I had to put out the fire."

"They were not on fire. Did you see fire?"

"Yes, I saw the flames. They were flames of hell. I had to beat the fire." Mary Jane spoke with such strength and certainty that Jesse stopped asking anymore questions..

It was a long hard trip to Oregon aboard a train to California then up the coast to Oregon. The family arrived in Portland then took a paddlewheel steamer up the Columbia to Ceilo Falls. There they disembarked and somehow got to The Dalles.

The Dalles was a boom town that had seen better days. At one point in time The Dalles was considered by Congress to be the location of a new mint after Denver. Legislation was passed and people were appointed to carry out the plan. Unfortunately a ship sank outside of San Francisco that carried supplies and the man who was to officially institute the mint. The hope of The Dalles sank with that ship.

Mary Jane, wife of Jesse, was essentially abandoned in The Dalles while Jesse went off hunting for gold. She took out her anger, sense of abandonment, and loneliness on the children. Paul was so badly beaten once that he bled from his ear for weeks. Fred hid from his mom and stole food in order to survive. The boys lived in fear of their mother. Mary Jane showed signs of psychosis. She talked to herself, imagined dangers that did not exist, and saw her children as the enemy at times. She complained constantly about Jesse and his "bad behavior." She could smell other women on his clothes.

Most of the time she experienced a sado-masochist feeling when she beat her children. She felt a near sexual pleasure in their screams and pain. It did not take too many   times of this abuse until Fred and Jesse just ran and hid.

"Where is mom?" said Fred.

"I don't know but she is on the warpath." Jesse sounded sympathetic.

"I think we better hide out for a couple of days." Jesse always had the best ideas.

After two days Mary Jane became frightened. She welcomed her boys back with open remorse.

She gave up on the fantasies of her husband and moved to Portland with her children. In the early 1900's. She found a new man. Jay Wing was the owner of a growing feed store in East Portland in the Lentz section of town near Mount Tabor. The boys, Fred and Paul, had a new father and it was a period of reprieve for them. The new family moved to Yakama where to boys went to High School and worked for their step- father who held together his new family. He had two more children with Mary Jane. Joseph and Francis kept Mary Jane's attention. She had less interest in the older boys. Besides, they were much bigger than her. The only power she had over them was psychological.

Jesse lived in Grant county Oregon for the next thirty years. At age 51 he picked up stakes and moved to Shasta County in southern Oregon. A small gold rush was underway but like his earlier life he was too late. Five years later he moved to Ada, Idaho, near Boise, home to another flare up of a gold rush. He died at age 77 in Ada.

Mary Jane took her sons to Portland where she met Jay Ring who owned a growing feed store in East Portland. Mary Jane was a woman who liked to be in control. For the first time in her life she met a man who could control her. She felt comfort in this knowledge. She also felt comforted by the stability that this man could provide her. It was such a contrast to her life with Jesse. She married this man and for a brief period they lived in Yakama, Washington, where Jay expanded his feed store empire. The boys took on the name of their new father.

The family moved back to Portland where Mary

Jane gave birth to two more children: Joseph and Francis. Mary Jane turned her attention to her new family. This gave Paul and Fred a reprieve. Besides, they were becoming big men who towered over their mother. During the early 30s Paul and Fred worked in their step-father's store. The effects of the depression did not touch this family.

"Boys, you are doing a good job." Jay said to Paul. "You are able to carry a 100 pound feed sack. I think it is time that you and your brother learn to operate the sacking machine." Jay had purchased a grain storage bin with an attached conveyer belt and funnel for sacking grain. He had also purchased a supply of hemp grain sacks. He patiently showed the boys how to hook the sacks on the mouth of the funnel. There were four hooks to keep the end of the sack open. When the sack was nearly full the operator had to pull a handle to stop the flow of grain a, lift the heavy sack off the hooks and hand it to another person who would sew the sack closed, and at the same time hook up another sack and released the bin handle to fill another sack.   All this had to be done without spilling too much grain. It was like a dance. I one step is missed or not done with precision and strength there would be a blinding mess to cleanup. Dust would fill the air and production would stop if a mistake was made.

A few times of trial and error were experienced. "Boys, boys, what is going on here" Jay would say as Paul and Fred scrambled to shut off a flow of grain onto the floor because a sack was not hung properly or the bin handle was not closed completely. "Ok boys, let's clean it up and start over again. We got customers waiting." He would say this with a slight laugh. He was so gentle with the boys. He knew what they had gone through with their mother. The boys loved him. They feared their mother.

Paul had to kill a armed man breaking into his home sometime in the late 1940. Paul evidently was devastated at having to kill another human being. It sent him into a spiral and he started self medicating with alcohol. Up to that point everyone knew him as a gentle giant (he was very tall with a stocky awkward frame) an actual description by neighbors. He evidently had a big heart and was the first to step forward to help someone in need.

Fred had anger management issue's stemming it

would appear from Jesse's abandonment of Mary and the boy's. Something that only got worse through the years.

The human condition is very complex. Human beings can be both cruel and compassionate at the same time. While Mary Jane could be cruel to her children she had a very compassionate public side. Mary was also known for her religious charity work. She had the ability to grow anything, and her canary aviary took up the whole upstairs attic.

Her husband Jay Wing only reinforced that charitable spirit, When the depression hit he built a rooming house on the farm on Foster Ave. and was able to put a lot of men to work. Mary started a huge community garden, she supplied the land, seeds and did much of the planting herself. It started small in the 1920's, (she had community gardens in both Yakima and Portland) She provided for her family or anyone else needing help to put food on the were warmly welcomed to receive of the garden. By 1930 the Portland garden was over an acre and a half, there were free range goats for milk and a bountiful fruit and veggie garden.

She and Jay couldn't and wouldn't allow their neighbors and other's to go hungry. By 1934 not only had they suffered their own monetary losses, but had been forced to sell all the real estate and store's in Yakima to support the general/feed store and garage in Lents.

Mary had started to see the toll it was taking on Jay, the family and business. Mary was up at 4:30 every morning cooking for up to 30 people, cleaned up, and went to the store to mind it, while Jay delivered the mail to anyone who couldn't get out. He was Post Master General of Lents from the 1890's to his death in 1935. As soon as he got back she would tend to the garden for an hour and then go start the noon meal, often making extra and taking meal packages to anyone who may have been in need. She was an excellent cook and could easily without thought or measure make meals for 100 people by herself.

Mary loved birds. She was the bird-lady of Lentz. She evidently had a natural skill as a chicken sexer....she could tell the sex of a newborn chick and she workerd for a group of huge chicken ranches in the area. She would leave before 4 am and wouldn't get home until sometimes 9 or 10 pm. She would take a bucket lunch and could sex 250 chicks in an hour. She started working at the age of 10, before school and after. Chick sexing is a fine art and she was in high demand. By 13 she was basically home schooled and worked on the ranches training migrating workers on the ranches and also sexing the chicks. When Jay died of sudden cardiac arrest, the store's, farm and garage were not in good financial shape.

Fred didn't want to remain in Portland. He bought a farm in Klamath Falls. And the burden fell on Paul.. His wife Amanda was well known for being very demeaning, mean spirited and sometimes down right cruel.

Mary evidently worked well into the night seven day's a week and was known for her tireless work in the community.

Jesse also moved to Klamath Falls. He lived with his son Fred and harvested Cascara bark. He was known as a ***BIG*** dreamer, and was very much a loner. And a little more than a bit of a womanizer...he was charming, good looking in a weathered sort of way.

He was an "an audacious story teller" who loved "whiskey and women". He evidently could spin a boring day into a wild adventure. He always had some kind of herding dog travelling with him and he couldn't stay put in one place for any length of time. He lived off the land and in harmony with the land. He didn't like four walls but was an excellent carpenter, builder that he learned from his father Martin. He had an imagination to create whatever he needed out of nothing. He would work for a local carpenter when he strolled into town, for pocket money and was known to have great skills; a perfectionist, and a very hard worker. Everyone whom he worked for loved him, but he just couldn't stay still.

Jay Ring died in 1935. His death caused an escalation in abuse of the children by Mary Jane. She screamed, beat, and abused the boys and especially the young daughter Francis. She called her a whore and vile names. The family scattered avoiding the company of their mother who was clearly suffering from hallucinations. Mary Jane retreated to the bottle. The voices became louder. Somehow at age 56 she found another man: Nels Borland. They moved across the Columbia River to Clark County..   Mary died in October 1971.

During the later years Paul and Fred built their lives and families in the Portland, Oregon, area. Paul was a grain salesman. His work for his step father in the feed store gave him the connections to become a first rate salesman. His affable character and wit along with his intelligence was a perfect combination for success. He had a patent for a feed pellet machine.

Paul saw how much feed was wasted by animals and farmers because grain was delivered and fed to cattle in a loose form. Paul figured that pellets would make the grain easier for the animals to eat and for the farmers to handle. He got the idea one day watching his wife Amanda make spagetti with an extruderr, combine it with a circular blade, add a binding agent, and one could process pellets. If the binding agent was some form of protien oil such as corn oil, this would add nutritional value to the product.

Paul tinkered the parts of machines until he had a pellet producing machine. Of course this out-raged Amanda. She took it out on the children. Paul was spending money on a patent attorney and dozens of machines that according to Amanda he was "ruining" the moment he got them.

"You are taking perfectly good nooble machines and ruining them. You take them apart and now they are good for nothing." Amanda looked like she was about to hit her husband.

Paul said, "You are just like my mother. There is no way to reason with you. I am creating something that will make us a fortune."

"It is putting us in the poor house." Amanda raged.

It is not uncommon for men who fear their abusive mothers to marry a woman who is like the woman they hate. It is a psychological phenomenon pregnant with irony.. We become (or marry) the thing we hate. An alcoholic will declare as an adult that he is not like his father but will develop an alcoholic personality of an alcoholic only without drinking. He will say that he is not like his alcoholic father because he does not drink but he will have the same temper, anti-social personality, and others will say he is just like his father. On the outside he may even be affable and charming but underneath there is fear and hatred that drives him.

Paul hid his pain as an abused child from others through humor and affability. Underneath was a vulnerable child who lived in fear of his mother. This created a personality type that attracted the very type of people he feared: mean, cruel women.

Amanda Grau was looking for a man like Paul, that is, someone she could control and dominate. Paul simply ran away and hid from her and his family as he did with his own mother. Paul was on the road as a sales man. This gave him the perfect excuse to leave whenever the tensions arose in the house where they lived in Lentz, Oregon, in East Portland.

One night when Paul was home Amanda woke up Paul.

"Did you here that?"

"What?" mumbled Paul.

"I hear someone downstairs."

"It is probably one of the boys."

"I don't think so" said Amanda. "I just checked on them."
Paul got up. He grabbed his shot gun and a couple of shells. He loaded the shells as he quietly walked barefoot downstairs. Shadow ran past him. It stopped. So did his heart. It felt like it was in his throat. He fired. The shot struck the shadow in the head. The sound of a body hitting the floor splashed across the room.

Paul did not remember much about what happened next. It seemed like a blur. All the lights in the house were turned on Amanda was screaming and yelling at the boys as they tried to get a peek at the body. Amanda called the police. Neighbors showed up asking questions about the noise. It took hours to remove the body. All Amanda could do was yell at Paul about the blood on the carpet and the broken lamp that got shattered in the spray of shot.

Paul was never the same afterwards. He grieved for the robber, the human being he had killed. He apologized to the robber's family not once but four times. He went to the funeral.

Paul was a big man. He was also slightly clumsy. His clumsiness increased. He seemed preoccupied. The police interviewed him and ruled it a justifiable homicide. The weight of guilt broke him.

He quit his job as a feed salesman, lost interest in inventing, and endured Amanda's nagging about the ruined carpet. He finally got another job selling Real Estate in Hillsboro just to get out of the house.

Amanda displayed a very cruel side toward her husband. She even blamed him for the killing. It deepened Paul's depression. Amanda seemed to have no empathic capacity. This psychopathic nature allowed her to torment her husband without remorse.

Chapter VII: Amanda

"Where are you kids" Amanda screamed. "It's Saturday and you have chores to do."

Lyle and Dorothy could hear their mother screaming as they were building a play fort in the backyard. "Dorothy, we should go inside."

Dorothy looked at her five year old brother. She could see the fear in his eyes. "Let's wait until she settles down."

It seemed as if their mother appeared out of nowhere. Dorothy was grabbed by the back of the neck, her mother beat her all the way back to the house. Amanda did not care if the neighbors were looking or could hear her threats to kill her daughter. Lyle trailed behind the screaming pair.

Lyle picked up the vodka bottle off the porch of the house as they all entered. Amanda disappeared into the bedroom with her daughter. Lyle could hear the dull thuds of a brutal beating. His mother opened the bedroom door and brushed past him. Lyle waited until he could hear his mother pacing in the kitchen then he entered the bedroom. His sister was bleeding from the head. There was a lump the size of a walnut on her forehead. "Come on Dorothy, let's go back to the fort and play."

Both of the children knew that after the storm in their mother's head was over that all was forgotten. Their mother returned to the bottle and as long as they stayed out of sight all would be well. It was a pattern that Lyle learned well. He saw his father display the same pattern. His father would come home from a sales trip, listen to his mother rage and complain to her husband, his father would listen and then leave again.

Back at the paly fort Lyle saw his sister fall down. She stiffened and shook. It was the first time but not the last time he saw his sister convulse in a seizure. It frightened him. He ran outside the fort. He saw a policeman walking up the steps of the house. The man knocked on the door. From a distance he could see his mother open the door. There was a brief exchange of very quiet words. Amanda collapsed sobbing.

Lyle was confused. He whispered to Dorothy,

"Dorothy, something is wrong with mother."

Dorothy was now sitting up. "I am so tired. What? What did you say?"

"Come on. There is a policeman at the house. Something is wrong with mother."

Jay Ring had dropped dead of a heart attack. The coroner had declared him dead and the body was taken to the city morgue. The coroner sent a police officer to the Ring house.

Paul Jr., Lyle, and Dorothy were recipients of the family psycho pathology of violence. In this generation it was even worse than previous generations. The type of woman Paul attracted was deeply disturbed. Psychosis and severe schizophrenic illness combined with a need to strike out against here own children was a near deadly combination, especially for Dorothy. Perhaps, because of self-hatred and because Dorothy was female, she became the target of extreme physical abuse. Dorothy suffered seizures from the physical beatings. This meant that she suffered brain injuries.

The monster of violence took several generations to create. It began with the development of men who were without roots. America was filled with men who felt dispossessed. John Vandenbrugen left his homeland and moved to America. His son left New York for the Midwest to begin again and create a new life in Kansas. His two youngest sons vacated their home for Colorado lured by the promised riches of the gold rush. These men created a restlessness within the male psyche. It caused a need for women who would punish them and demand stability. At a deep level these men knew they were risking a stable life for their families.

Amanda Grau Vandenbrugen was my grandmother. My father, Lyle, committed suicide in 1959. It is possible I could have been left in her care. It is possible I could have been a recipient of this family tradition of violence. Fortunately I was taken from this family and adopted into a new family. The legacy of violence was broken.

Chapter VIII: Lorraine and Edna

Lyle was my father. As a teenager he was timid and shy according to his schoolmates. He did not have many friends. He lived in fear of his mother and stayed as far away from home as possible. Since the death of his stepfather the family fell into a deep silence. His mother medicated her grief with alcohol. She never talked to Lyle or his older brother Paul except to have them run down to the store on Foster Road and get her more vodka. Dorothy took most of the abuse directed at the children. Lyle kept to himself until one day when he met Edna. Edna was a wild child who already had several run-in with the local police. She met Lyle when she was 12 years old. Lyle was on leave for a few weeks. Lyle had joined the Navy. He had just finished his training and was awaiting orders for his assignment.

Edna acted out sexually. Her mother was mentally ill and in the psychiatric facility in Troutdale. Lyle and Edna found respite and refuge in each other. Legally it was rape and pedophilia at work in the relationship. Lyle was ten years older than Edna. Lyle was afraid to approach women his own age. Instead he victimized Edna who was quite willing to participate in deviant sexual activities with Lyle. Lyle was reacting to the abuse he had felt at the hands of his mother.

Memory of the trauma executed by a domineering mother can crush a man into timidity, a kind of timidity that leads to preying on those weaker. Psychiatric literature is full of accounts of children like this who torture dogs, start fires, and act out sexually.

This is not the only way a child can react to a domineering mother but it was the way Lyle reacted.

Lyle returned to San Diego while Edna had her first child at age 13. After Lyle's first cruise he returned to Portland and Edna. Soon a second child was on the way. Lyle was away when his second child was born. Back in San Diego he met and married Lorraine. It was a shock to Edna when Lyle showed up and asked for the babies. Lyle had been reassigned to Tacoma. He had not done well in his Navy assignments. Instead of discharging him, Lyle was given one more chance and assigned to temporary duty at the Port of Tacoma. He took with him his wife Lorraine and petitioned a judge in Portland for custody of his children.

The two babies, Lyle Jr. (12 months) and Frances (1 month) were given to Lyle. The babies were in the care of Edna's mother who had been released from the work farm in Troutdale which served as a mental hospital for Multnomah County. Edna could not cope nor did she want to cope with two screaming babies. She signed the papers giving custody to Lyle and his new bride.

Infants who are severely deprived of basic emotional nurture, even though physically well cared for, can fail to thrive and can eventually die. Babies with less severe emotional deprivation can grow into anxious and insecure children who are slow to develop and who have low self-esteem. These children often show destructive behavior, angry acts (such as fire setting and animal cruelty), withdrawal, poor development of basic skills, alcohol or drug abuse, suicide, difficulty forming relationships and unstable job histories. Also, these children often grow up to become parents who abuse their own children, either emotionally or otherwise, due to the child's development being impaired in all domains of functioning. Unless the cycle is broken and unless these children are removed from such environments and placed into environments before the age of three the imprint of this kind of deprivation is stamped deeply into their psychological persona..

This type of trauma does not impact all children in the same way. Some children seem to be able to withstand the trauma. Others are crushed and live a lifetime of misery.

The small family moved to Tacoma into a small Navy apartment on south 38th street. It was a miserable situation for Lorraine.

"Would you please change the diapers on these kids?" Lorraine shouted at Lyle as he walked in the door from a long 24 hour day of work. Lyle had had guard duty.

"Just a minute" he said.

While Lyle was in the bathroom, Lorraine threw on her coat and slammed the door behind her. She never returned.

Lyle spent several days looking for Lorraine in downtown Tacoma.   He was reported AWOL by the Navy. He ran out of   money as the Navel fined him and took away one rank.   He found a job as a butcher but his long work hours led to complaints from his neighbors. His two boys were hungry and the crying forced the neighbors to call the authorities.

One evening, Lyle returned home to find two social workers waiting for him. The next day the Sherriff arrived at his work and gave him papers to sign.   They demanded his apartment key and when he returned home that night his boys were gone.

Lyle made several calls to the Lutheran Welfare agency in Tacoma. He was told that his boys were in an orphanage on Second Ave. in downtown Seattle. The next weekend he went with his sister Dorothy to the orphanage next to the Smith Tower. There they were reunited with the boys. An agreement was worked out to release the boys into temporary foster care with Dorothy. This worked for a while but the situation became overwhelming.   Dorothy suffered from seizures probably as a result of the beatings her mother gave her. When this condition was discovered the boys were taken back to the orphanage in downtown Seattle.

Chapter IX: Adoption

The two Vandenbrugen babies stayed at the temporary orphanage in Seattle until 1953. Lyle Jr. was featured on the front page of the Seattle Times as the face of the Seattle Christmas Fund. Tears streaming down his face caught the attention of the Smith family in Mount Vernon. Mrs. Smith who had suffered the death of an infant daughter and the diagnosis of "Mongolism" in her son and a recommendation to send him to a state institution, led her to desire the boy she saw in the newspaper. Her husband was a dairy farmer in the Skagit Valley. They did not have much money but they wanted to try and adopt the boy. A woman in their congregation at Salem Lutheran Church was a social worker. Mrs. Smith asked the social worker to help. Soon the boy in the newspaper arrived in the Skagit Valley for a trial visit in the Smith home.

Little was known about the baby Lyle Jr. He was a fat baby born at 10 pounds 6 ounces. The Smiths were told that Lyle had been abandoned with his younger brother. The brother suffered from "rickets, a medical condition die to lack of vitamin C.

They had been rescued from an apartment in Tacoma, restored to health, and were waiting for adoption. There was mention of an aunt who also was seeking custody.

The Smiths filed adoption papers for both children after six months. They returned to the orphanage and brought the second son home. The boys were renamed Dale and Dennis. A judge changed their names and hid their former identities. They became the sons of Mr. And Mrs. Albert and Martha Smith with the full rights and responsibilities as parents to the boys.

The legacy of violence was broken with the adoption. In a sense, Calvin was proved wrong. We, as humans are not born evil, depraved, or wicked. It appears that we may be born with certain tendencies or even diseases of mental illness or genetic predispositions to anger, depression, or mental retardation. Our environments allow or constrict the expression of these capacities or tendencies. Both nature and nurture are a play in the human character there is no doubt.

Of the Vandenbrugen boys, one turned out to be a citizen of the world founding humanitarian organizations and serving refugees in Iraq, earthquake victims in Haiti, and migrants in China. The other boy ended up suffering from psychosis, depression, and the consequences of self-medication. Still a change in the environment can help overcome conditioning. The negative social consequences of genetic conditions can be modified and give a person a chance to contribute to society in a positive way rather than end up in prison, psychiatric wards, or and early grave.

There is hope for those who suffer inter-generational violence. It requires radical change and most of all it requires love.

Afterward

I am the eldest of the two Vandenbrugen babies. I have never had an interest in searching for my past. I believe that the people who love you and raise you are your REAL parents. Parentage has nothing to do with biology. It has everything to do with love. For this reason and this reason alone, I had no interest in my genetic history, that is, until my daughter as an adult asked me about her genetic heritage.

I could not answer her. I did not know. So together we looked. It led us to a Vandenbrugen aunt by marriage. She had little interest in the family history but it did satisfy my daughter's questions.

Now after sixty years a genealogical researcher is providing me information on my family history. The dark face of family violence has shown itself in the light of this research. I am not angry and I am not sad. In fact, I am grateful that I was rescued.

As a child I had a sense of being rescued. I loved the stories of rescued children. The story of Moses, King Arthur, and Oedipus Rex reminded me of my own situation where I was taken away from my birth family and raised by shepherds and farmers.. I somehow knew that if I looked into my biological past that it would be a Pandora's Box filled with misery and evil. Maybe I had an unconscious memory of abuse and abandonment. Maybe an inherited phantom of violence was whispering to my soul and warning me. For whatever reason, I did not go down that path. Because I did not open that psychological box I can say with full gratitude "thank you" to me rescuers, the people who raised me,

Like John Wesley who was saved from a devastating house fire as a child and I can say with him "I was saved as a brand from the fire." This sense of salvation led Wesley to develop a deep religious sense. In the same manner I too have developed a deep religious sense. Today I am a priest and humanitarian. I have built school for thousands of children, trained thousands of teachers, developed orphanages, and organized rescue mission for abandoned children in Haiti, Iraq, and the Dominican Republc. I have established schools for "left behind migrant children in China

Geneology

Cornelius Vandenbrugen – Arrived in America 1760
Farmer: Fought in Battle of Lexington, 1777. Assigned two lots (198, 104) Lansingburgh, NY

John Vandenbrugen – 1796-?   Schodack, Rensselaer, NY
Farmer: Fought at Battle of Plattsburgh, 9/11/1813.

Martin Vandenbrugen – 1832-1912 Schodack, NY
Carpenter. Moved to KS. Fought in Missouri/Kansas border wars.

Jesse Vandenbrugen – 1874-1951 Grasshopper Falls, KS
Gold Miner. Moved to Teller, CO., The Dalles, OR., Shasta, OR, Ada, ID.

Paul Vandenbrugen – 1902-1975 El Paso, Colorado
Feed salesman and Inventor: East Portland, Lentz District.

Lyle Vandenbrugen – 1929-1959 Portland, Oregon
Navy veteran: committed suicide Multnomah County Jail.

Lyle Vandenbrugen Jr. - 1950- San Diego CA Naval Hospital: adoptee: Writer, priest, humanitarian.

Other books by Dale A. Johnson

Available at Amazon.com, Barnes and Noble, and Lulu.com/barhanna, distributor of the New Sinai imprint.

Science Books
1. Anachrology
2. An Incomplete Guide to Small Blue Butterflies of Southwestern China
3. An Incomplete Guide to the Butterflies of the Dominican Republic
4. Field Notes on Martian Life
5. Einstein at Prayer, Jesus in the Lab

Detective Series
6. Columbia River Murders
7. Mahjong Murders
8. Laowai Murders
9. Guan Yin Murders
10. Mahjong Murder Mystery Series

Fiction
11. Festschrift of Fiction
12. Little Stories from the Monastery Between the Mountain and the Sea
13. Twin of Jesus
14. Stories of the Temple between the Mountain and the Sea
15. Syncretism: Creativity and Consciousness in the Tang Dynasty
16. Women without Faces

Humanitarian Studies
17. Release the Hero Within
18. Why Should We Care?
19. Altruism: Serving Others

Cookbook
20. The Great Fast Cookbook

Monastic Studies
21. A Rule for Community

History
22. Following the Sun
23. Visits of Gertrude Bell to Tur Abdin
24. Chronicle of Joshua of Zuqnin
25. Asian Jesus in China
26. Asian Jesus
27. Asian Christ
28. Asian Christian
29. The Asian Faces of Jesus

30. Following the Sun
31. Monk George and his Debate with Muslims
32. Jing Jiao: Luminist Religion of China
33. Luminous Stones: Christian Inscriptions in Ancient China
Inspirational
34. Wake Up! Pay Attention
35. Release the Hero Within
36. Your Life is None of Your Business
     Published in Chinese:Life is None of Your Business (China Edition)
37. Lives of Gratefulness
38. Forty Meditations by Father Dale
39. Bamboo Dreams
40. Hospitality
Barhanna Monograph Series
41. Barhanna Monograph Series
     42. The Syriac Codex Computers
     43. The Goodspeed Syriac Fragments
     44. Syriac Fragments of MS. Balamand 15
     45. The Jesus Caves of China
     46. Arab Christian Art of Balamond
47. Barhanna Monographs, Vol. 2

Biography
48. Fire on the Mountain
49. Is God Dead Yet? I hope so!
Syriac Studies
50. Syriac Genius
51. Syriac Influences in Western History
52. Living as a Syriac Palimpsest
     Republished as: Dominican Palimpsest
53. Syriac Studies
54. Asian Christ
55. A Gospel Harmony
56. Daily Prayers from the Language of Jesus
57. Tracts on the Mountain of the Servants   (hagiography)
58. Divine Liturgy of the West Syriac Traditions
59. Ancient Aramaic Hymns of Christianity
60. Monks of Mount Izla
61. Corpus Gradum
     62. Hilaria: A Woman Who Became a Man

Intra-religion Studies
63. Christ Mind, Buddha Heart
64. Jesus on the Silk Road: Essays on Christianity in China, Mongolia, and Asia Minor
65. Soft Like Water
66. A Disciple of the Pear Garden
67. Wisdom is Not What You Think

Recent Books
68. Searching for Jesus on the Silk Road – paperback, history
69. The Lost Churches of the Silk Road – Hardcover, history
70. Remembering the Future – Science Fiction
71. Treasures of Tur'Abdin – Art analysis
72. The Greatest Manchu Painting – Art History
73. The Emperor's Regret - Short Stories, fiction
74. Airpocalypse – Coming Soon to an Environment Near You - Science

Jesee Keller Vandenburg (b. 1876 Grasshopper Falls, KS. d. 12-25-1951 Ada, ID)
Model for Jesse Vandenbrugen
Husband to Mary Jane (1878-1971)

Mary Jane Vandenburg (b. Missouri, d. Multnomah, OR.)
model for Mary Jane Vandenbrugen
Husband to Jesse

Paul and Fred Vandenburg
Models for Paul and Fred Vandenbrugen
Children of Jesse and Mary Jane
Photo from 1916.
Brothers were born 1902 and 1904 El Paso, CO.
Paul died in 1975 Hillsboro and Fred 1976
Portland.